MW00905405

© 2020 By Stephen Daingerfield Dunn All rights reserved.

This book or any portion thereof may not be reproduced or used in any

manner whatsoever without express written permission of the author.

Printed in the United States of America

First edition, 2020 http://poemsforme.com

ISBN # 978-1-0879-4526-2

BUG DRIAMS

WRITTEN BY

S. DAINGERFIELD DUNN

ILLUSTRATED BY

MARY MADDUX

I saw a tiny bug
all shiny and green
and then I saw him wink
as strange as that might seem

We shared a little wish

Me and Mr. Green

Where could we find others

who have the same dreams?

we invited the palegray moth
who lit upon the light

But he could care less

As he quickly took flight

Then there was Mr. Mouse
who did just what he did
scampered from room to room
Scaring all the kids

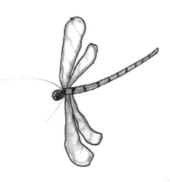

Shortly after that
A robin came along
Winking once again
Singing his springtime song

He frightened the little bug
who hid beneath the door
Knowing that the bird
Was not to be ignored

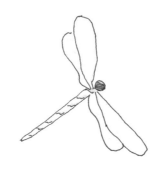

Once he had flown
We continued on our road
thinking we might ask
the warty, slimy toad

However once again
The bug feared for his life
the toad with the tongue
Brought the teeny insect strife

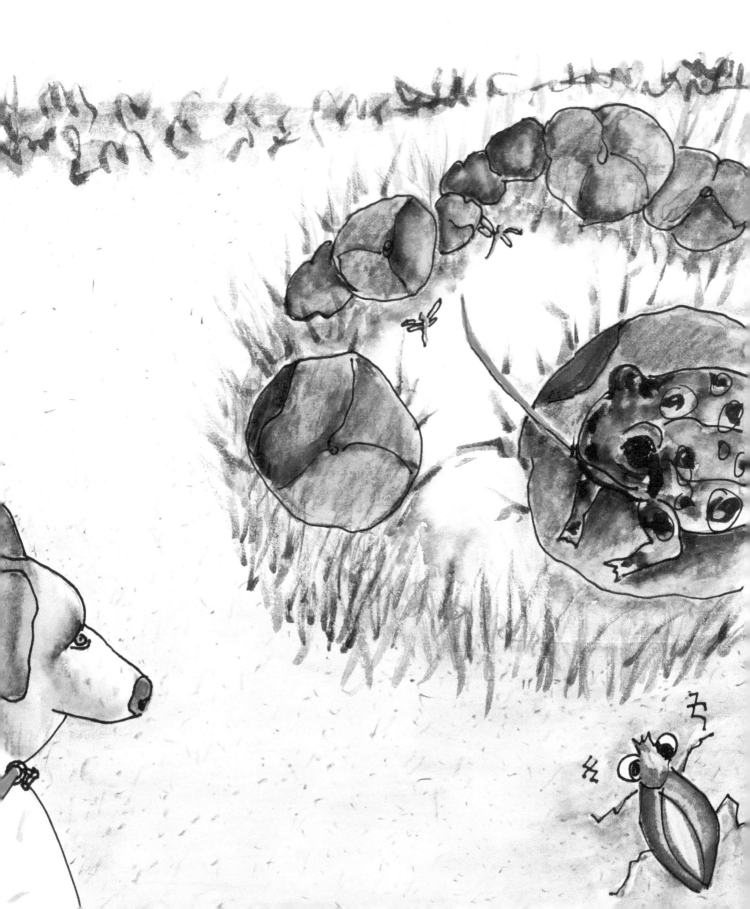

Changing our path
To avoid the froggy pond
We traveled the world over
And places far beyond

We searched for our dreams
Gave it our all
the bug found a lot
Because he was so small

They spoke to the French
And said "we we"
However the Parisians first thought
Was that they had to pee pee!

the dreams that we found
were of many shapes and sizes
Most quietly hidden
in very many disguises

I on the other hand
wanted only the best
Refused to take a nap
Did not want to rest

But the thing we discovered
Between the bug and myself
Was a love for one another
A dream unto its self

Seems that our long search
into the unknown
Could have come to a happy ending
Right here in our own home ...

... THE END

A resident of Dallas, Texas, **S. Daingerfield Dunn** is an award-winning interior designer with over 30 years experience in the design industry at the helm of Stephen Dunn Designs. He has also had an extensive career as a noted hairdresser and owner of two of the most exclusive beauty salons in Dallas, Texas. S. Daingerfield Dunn is also the owner of the decorative window furnishings company Le Corniche, and a one-of-a-kind pillow firm called Beauregarde.

Mr. Dunn has been honored by DHome magazine and the Dallas Design Center as one of city's best designers for 12 consecutive years. His homes have been featured in publications nation-wide, and his work cited as "...the most interesting house in the Metroplex".

Stephen's diverse interests include travel, art collecting/painting, entertaining and cooking, dancing and good conversation. He has performed for the past 5 years in the Spectacular Follies at Dallas's Eisenmann Theater. He serves on the board of the humanitarian group KinDship, and for four years has volunteered his design talents as member of the board of Unity Church of Dallas, overseeing renovations and the Unity landscape program.

He is married to his partner of 39 years, Mr. Beau Black, who Stephen describes as a "force unto himself " in the Dallas Design Center – and life itself! Their home is ruled by two furry children, Camilla and FiFi Fiona!

To date, he has published 8 books of poetry and another children's book, "A Day in the Life of a Raindrop". His first book "A Little Boy From Nowhere Texas" won first prize in its category from the Texas Association of Authors in 2017. Stephen launched his poetry career in 2012 and to date he has composed over 2,600 poems. To be continued...

Mary Maddux, is an artist who lives in Dallas, TX. She has worn many hats in the role of artist, from creating special finishes and murals to portraits of pets and children.

Bug Dreams is her first venture into illustration. She was immediately enamored by the characters and couldn't wait to capture their stories, (journey).

Scout, the narrator, is a Jack Russell mix, who wishes she could have all of the adventures in the book.

The bug chooses to remain anonymous.